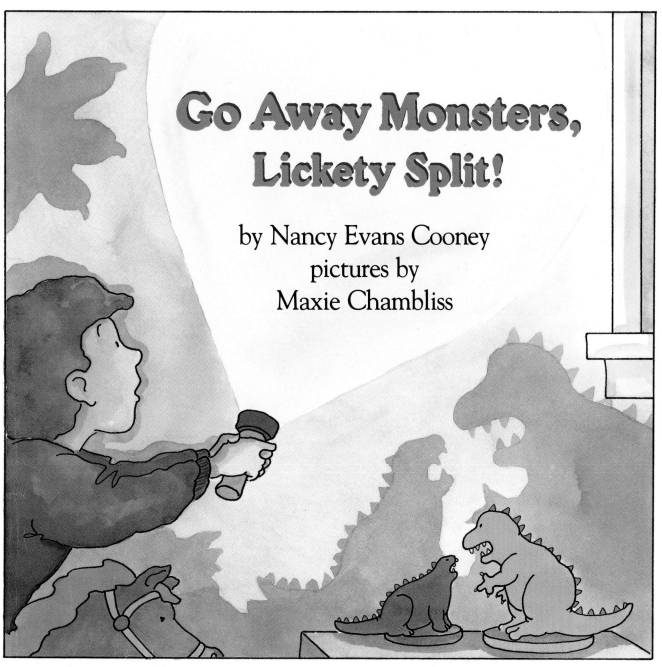

Go Away Monsters, Lickety Split!

by Nancy Evans Cooney
pictures by
Maxie Chambliss

G. P. Putnam's Sons   New York

For Carolyn and Bob—N.E.C.

For Grandmother and Grandpop Sweet—M.C.

Text copyright © 1990 by Nancy Evans Cooney.
Illustrations copyright © 1990 by Maxie Chambliss.
All rights reserved. This book, or parts thereof, may
not be reproduced in any form without permission
in writing from the publisher.
G. P. Putnam's Sons, a division of The Putnam &
Grosset Group, 200 Madison Avenue, New York,
NY 10016.
Published simultaneously in Canada.
Printed in Hong Kong by South China Printing Co.
(1988) Ltd.
Book design by Christy Hale.

Library of Congress Cataloging-in-Publication Data
Cooney, Nancy Evans. Go away monsters, lickety split!
Summary: Jeff is afraid of the monsters that might
be lurking in the dark when he goes to bed, until his
new kitten shows him the way to be brave.
[1. Bedtime—Fiction. 2. Night—Fiction. 3. Fear—
Fiction. 4. Cats—Fiction] I. Chambliss, Maxie, ill.
II. Title.
PZ7.C7843Go 1990 [E] 89-10515
ISBN 0-399-21935-8
10 9 8 7 6 5 4 3 2 1
First Impression

After the movers left, Jeffrey unpacked his toys in his new bedroom. He reached up and sat his stuffed pig on top of his bookcase. "There!" he said, "You can watch over my room for me."

He looked around and smiled. Everything was in place.

Now he could help his mother find the pots and
pans because he was getting hungry.

But his mother had a better idea. "Let's get Dad and
go out for a quick hamburger before we unpack."

Later, Jeffrey pulled the kitchen things out of the boxes so his mother could put them away. But he was so tired he fell asleep on the kitchen floor right in the middle of helping.

The next morning Jeffrey woke up in his bed with sunshine pouring in the window. After breakfast he looked around the yard. He had never had so much room to play outside. His father was working in the garage. "I'll help you, Dad," Jeffrey said. They played hide-and-seek while they worked.

That night Jeffrey noticed how dark and quiet it was, not at all like their apartment in the city. There were no lights shining through the windows from signs and cars and streetlights. There was no noise from sirens and traffic and neighbors.

The new house had a long hallway with dark doorways on both sides. No telling *what* might be hiding in the shadows.

At bedtime, Jeffrey took a deep breath.

Then, he hurried by the big bedroom before a monster could leap out.

He rushed past the bathroom because a monster might be lurking there.

He raced into his bedroom and flicked on the light.
Suppose a monster was hiding in the dark?

Jeffrey jumped into bed.

His mother came in to kiss him good night. She turned off the light and went out, closing the door behind her.

Jeffrey was alone—or was he?

He tucked his ears under the covers so he couldn't hear anything strange.

He squeezed his eyes shut so he couldn't see anything strange.

He left just his nose out of the covers so he could breathe.

Then he lay very still and tried to forget what might be around him in the dark.

But it didn't work.

"Mom!"

"What is it?" his mother asked.

Jeffrey whispered, "It's scary here in the dark. Please leave the door open."

"I'll leave the hall light on tonight, too. But tomorrow, suppose we get some night-lights?"

"Thanks, Mom."

The next day they plugged a light in the hallway, one in the bathroom, and another in his room.

That night Jeffrey felt better until he saw that those lights cast scary shadows. He wasn't sure they helped at all.

The next day his father asked, "How do you like the house?"

And Jeffrey said, "Fine."

"How do you like your room?"

"Fine."

"Mom told me you think it's too dark at night. Would you like this flashlight to carry with you?"

"Sure! Thanks."

That night Jeffrey's heart still thumped as he scurried down the hall even though the night-light was on. He turned on his bedroom light and looked around. Everything was in place.

Then he switched off the light. Everything vanished. He turned on his new flashlight, but it lit only a small spot and his room seemed even darker.

Jeffrey stood still. What else was in the room with him?

He switched the bedroom light back on. No monster
was there—*this* time.

But on most nights—even with the night-lights and
the flashlight and the hall light—he still ran fast to his
room and he stayed awake a long time before falling asleep.

On Sunday his grandmother came to visit.

"I brought Jeffrey a present for the new house." She placed a big basket on the living room floor and carefully lifted out a little kitten.

As soon as it touched the floor, the kitten ran straight to Jeffrey. Everyone laughed as the kitten climbed into his lap and started licking his chin.

"I think she likes you, Jeffrey!" his father said. "She really ran to you lickety-split."

"What's lickety-split?" Jeffrey asked.

"It means very fast."

"I'll name her Lickety because she sure licks, too."

At bedtime, Lickety ran right ahead of Jeffrey. Down
the hall they went—not even glancing into the other
rooms. She marched straight toward Jeffrey's bedroom.

Except for the light from the hall the room was
dark. But Lickety didn't care.

She paused and moved her head around with her
nose in the air, as if sniffing for monsters. So Jeffrey
did, too.

With her ears alert, Lickety cocked her head to
one side as though listening for monsters. So Jeffrey
listened hard, too.

Lickety explored the floor. She didn't bump into
anything. Jeffrey explored, too.

Finally, Lickety jumped on the bed and curled into a tiny ball.

Jeffrey patted her and whispered, "Don't worry. I'll protect you."

He turned on the light for one last look around.
Jeffrey got into bed and said, "Go away, monsters,
lickety-split!"

Then he snapped off the light and went to sleep.